r/ 4.5
pt 2.0

Dear Mom and Dad and Philip,
   I miss you very, very, very much.
I want to come home. I still don't
like camp, except for Skye and Daisy and
the baby birds and campfire. I like the
nurse, too.

Dear
   y
butt
of
are

Beany Goes to Camp

For inspiring me with your precious letters home from camp, thank you, Mary!

For sharing camp ideas and memories, thanks to Joel Wojciechowski, Laura Wolfe, Suzannah Emmons, and the students at the following schools: Albion Primary (NY), Brookville Middle School (OH), Centerville Elementary (PA), Governor Mifflin Intermediate (PA), Halifax Elementary (PA), St. Eleanor (PA), St. John the Evangelist (NY), Sanford School (DE), and York Township Elementary (PA).

For allowing me to spend an afternoon absorbing the flavor of camp life, thanks to Camp Cory on Keuka Lake, Penn Yan, NY.

Beany Goes to Camp

Susan Wojciechowski

illustrated by

Susanna Natti

CANDLEWICK PRESS
CAMBRIDGE, MASSACHUSETTS

To my godchildren, Timothy, Brett, Amanda, and Evan.
You'll always have a special place in my heart.
S. W.

★

To my golden cousins the Stephanio girls,
Dinah, Carol, Ellie, Laura, and remembering Mary Ann.
S. N.

Text copyright © 2002 by Susan Wojciechowski
Illustrations copyright © 2002 by Susanna Natti

First edition 2002

Library of Congress Cataloging-in-Publication Data

Wojciechowski, Susan.
Beany goes to camp / Susan Wojciechowski ;
illustrated by Susanna Natti. — 1st ed.
p.   cm.
Summary: Beany definitely does not want to spend her summer
vacation at camp, but she endures bugs and a bossy cabin-mate,
finds a new friend, and has an okay time after all.
ISBN 0-7636-1615-X
[1. Camps—Fiction. 2. Vacations—Fiction. 3. Friendship—Fiction.
4. Humorous stories.] I. Natti, Susanna, ill. II. Title.
PZ7.W8183 Bdf 2002
[Fic]—dc21   2001035045

2 4 6 8 10 9 7 5 3 1

Printed in the United States of America

This book was typeset in MBembo.
The illustrations were done in pen and ink.

Candlewick Press
2067 Massachusetts Avenue
Cambridge, Massachusetts 02140

visit us at www.candlewick.com

Contents

★ ★ ★
★ ★
★

Arrival

★ ★ ★
★ ★ ★

On the first day of summer vacation, I wrote this in my journal:

> Vacation is for
>   sleeping late, watching TV,
> riding my bike, eating popsicles,
> reading
>   Vacation is NOT for
> GOING TO CAMP!

That's why, one Sunday in August, even though my dad sat in the car honking the horn and yelling, "All aboard! Next stop Camp Onondaga," I didn't get in the car. I lay on my bed with my stuffed moose, Jingle Bell, wishing I could disappear so I wouldn't have to go to camp.

If I disappeared, my parents would come into my room and think I ran away. That would show them. They'd get all scared and say, "Why did we make Beany sign up for camp? If only she'd come back home, we'll never make her go to camp." Then I'd make myself appear and everything would be fine.

But nothing like that happened. My dad kept honking the car horn till finally Mom came into my room and asked if I was ready to go.

"No," I mumbled into Jingle Bell's fur.

"Let's go over the checklist one more time," she said, and read a list of stuff I was supposed to have packed in my duffel bag, like sweatshirt, rain parka, toothbrush, seven changes of underwear, sunscreen, insect repellent, bathing suit, towels. Every time she read an item, I sort of grunted. I wasn't really listening, though.

Finally Mom pushed my legs over and sat down on the edge of my bed. "I know you

don't want to go, Beany," she said. "But sometimes parents really know what's best. I know you'll have a wonderful time at camp."

"I hate camp," I said.

"How can you hate camp? You've never been to camp."

"My friend Julie told me she got a tenth-degree sunburn at camp," I said.

"There's no such thing as a tenth-degree sunburn. Besides, you've got sunscreen."

"Camp is dumb," I said.

"Carol Ann doesn't think so," Mom answered. "Carol Ann liked camp so much last summer she's going back. Just think. When you get there, you'll already know one person."

That did not make me feel better. I was mad at my friend Carol Ann. She was the one who gave my mom the idea about me going to camp. One day in the spring Carol Ann came to my house and started talking about Camp Onondaga. She told my mom and me that she had gone there the year before and had a great time. Then she put a folder full of stuff telling about Camp Onondaga on the table. I tried to grab it, but my mom beat me to it. When she looked through it and said, "Hmmm," I knew I was in trouble.

Now Mom was rubbing my back and saying, "I'll make a deal with you. If you don't like camp, you'll never have to go again. But you have to promise me you won't go there with your mind made up that you'll have a miserable time. Give camp a chance."

So I got in the car with my parents and my big brother, Philip, and we drove the two-hour trip to Camp Onondaga. My brother, who's thirteen and has been to camp, told me things I should know.

"Here's the great thing about going to camp," he said, quietly, so my parents wouldn't hear. "Mom and Dad won't be there. You'll have one whole week of no parents telling you what to do. You can eat junk food whenever you want. You can

drink all the soda you want without Mom shaking her head and telling you it'll rot your teeth. You can wear the same pair of socks every day."

"Yuck," I said. "Why would I want to do that?"

"Okay, bad example," said Philip "but I'll tell you the most fun thing of all—playing tricks on your cabin counselor. Like, when she's in the shower, everybody turns on all the hot-water faucets at once and the shower water turns ice cold. Or, at night, you put a snake in her bed."

That's when I screamed, right at the back of my dad's head.

Dad yelled, "What in blazes is going on back there? Do you want me to get in an accident?"

"Philip says there are snakes at camp!"

"Philip," Dad said, frowning at my

brother in the rearview mirror, "If you'd like me to pull over and let you walk the rest of the way, just keep it up."

When we turned onto a bumpy dirt road with a sign, Welcome to Camp Onondaga, I started to bite my nails. Dad parked the car, and we went into a building called Mess Hall, where everyone had to fill out forms.

Mom squeezed my shoulder and said, "Relax." That was easy for her to say. She was going to get back in the car and go home to eat in her own house and sleep in her own bed and not get attacked by a snake.

While my family looked at a bulletin board full of pictures taken at camp last year, I took a bunch of forms to a long table and started to fill them in. First I filled in my name: Bernice Sherwin-Hendricks. I'm named Bernice after my great-grandmother, and Sherwin-Hendricks because my mom stuck her name onto my dad's when they got married. Most people call me Beany, though, except for my brother. Sometimes he calls me Beanhead. I do not like that one bit.

Then I filled in address, phone number, and birth date. For the line marked *allergies,* I was thinking about filling in *camp,* when all of a sudden I heard a loud voice yell, "Beany!" It was Carol Ann. She had spotted me from two tables away and was running over to me.

"This week is going to be so fun! I hope we're in the same cabin!" she said, jumping up and down with her fingers crossed. I tried to ignore her. Carol Ann is my best friend because we live on the same street and ride the school bus together, but some-

times I don't like her that much. She is very bossy and acts like she knows everything in the whole world, just because she is four months and six days older than me.

"See you later," Carol Ann said and went running to another table where I heard her yell out, "Megan! This week is going to be so fun!"

The next thing I had to do was check off which activities I wanted to do from a long list. Campers get a choice, except for swimming; everybody has to take swimming lessons. It was hard to pick activities because I didn't like most of the choices, like volleyball, basketball, and tennis. I'm scared of balls coming at me. I ended up choosing arts-and-crafts because it sounded like fun, and archery because the word sounded nice, even though I didn't know what it meant. Then Dad looked at a map they gave us, and we found the cabin I was assigned to.

Every cabin had an Indian name. Mine was called Mohawk. It was at the end of the row of girls' cabins. Each cabin had a little porch on it with a wooden bench. Inside were four bunk beds and one regular bed in the corner for the counselor. The counselor got a dresser. The eight campers just got big nails in the wall for hanging their clothes. There was a bulletin board next to the door

with a big smiley face and the word *Welcome* tacked up on it.

I picked out a bunk near the brightest window because somebody told me once that bugs like the dark. I was glad there was a lower bunk free—the upper bunks were probably full of cobwebs. Then Mom and Dad hugged me goodbye. Philip punched my arm and reminded me about the shower trick. Then they left. I pulled Jingle Bell out of my duffel bag and lay on my bunk, rubbing his ear. Sometimes that helps me feel better.

I was alone for about one minute, when Carol Ann came running into the cabin, jumped on top of me and started to tickle my sides. "Yay," she yelled, right in my ear. "We got the same cabin!"

She pulled me off the bed and dragged me outside to show me the bathrooms, the showers, the boys' cabins, and a big area where campfires would be held, one on Tuesday and one on the last night. Then we went together to the mess hall for supper. I think it's called a mess hall because it's the place for eating, and everybody is allowed to eat messy at camp.

After corn on the cob, hamburgers, and watermelon, the camp director stood up and blew a loud whistle that made everybody stop talking.

"What's the best camp in the world?" the director asked.

"Camp Onondaga!" lots of kids yelled.

"Who are the best campers in the world?" she asked.

"We are!" the kids yelled back.

"And for those of you who've been here before, let's show the newcomers our camp cheer."

Onondaga, Onondaga, is the best,
Better than, better than, all the rest.
Say it as you stamp your feet, Onondaga.
Say it as you clap your hands, Onondaga.
Say it quiet as a mouse, Onondaga.
Say it proud, yell it loud, Onondaga.
Louder than you did before, Onondaga.
Loudest that your voice can roar,
ONONDAGA!

Then they all cheered and screamed.

"Camp Onondaga welcomes you," the camp director said. She told us all the rules about what time we had to get up in the morning (early) and be at the flagpole for the pledge, and what time we had to be at the flagpole at night to bring down the flag, and be ready for "lights out" at night. She told us that each cabin would get points during the week for things like having clean cabins and doing jobs well and having team spirit and participating in events.

"At the end of the week," she said, "the cabin with the most points will be named Cabin of the Week. All of us on the staff—the counselors, the cooks, the nurse, the teachers—will be watching you and recording points. So go for it!"

She dismissed us, and we all went to our cabins for a cabin meeting. We sat on the floor in a circle. Carol Ann made sure she sat right next to our cabin counselor, Daisy.

Daisy wore purple and white polka-dot nail polish. She told us she was going to school to learn how to be a hairstylist. Then she asked each of us to say our name. Besides Carol Ann and me, the other girls were Megan, Kwaneesha, Jocelyn, Victoria (who said we should call her Tory), Fiona (who said we absolutely should not call her

Fifi), and Skye. When I said my name, Daisy said she couldn't hear me, so I had to say it again.

The last girl was Skye, a girl I had spotted the minute I came into the cabin after supper. She had been curled up facing the wall on the bunk next to mine, not moving. Her hair was kind of weird. It was in ponytails, but the part was all crooked and was way

over to one side, so one of the ponytails had hardly any hair in it.

At the meeting, Skye had to say her name twice, too, before Daisy could hear it, then she started to cry. Daisy went over and put her arm around Skye. "It's okay, hon," she told her. I liked the way Daisy called Skye "hon" and put her arm around her. She kept her arm around Skye while she had each of us take a turn telling why we came to Camp Onondaga.

"I came to see all my friends from last year," said Kwaneesha.

"I came because I love to swim every day," said Megan.

"I like getting away from my brother for a week," said Fiona. Everybody laughed.

"I love absolutely everything about camp," Carol Ann said.

When it was my turn, I said, "I came

because my parents made me." Some girls laughed. I didn't like that. Skye didn't say why she came to camp. Daisy didn't make her.

Next, Daisy told us that she would list our jobs each day on the cabin bulletin board. We would have to do stuff like clearing the tables after meals, cleaning the bathrooms, and sweeping the cabin porch.

"The last thing we have to take care of tonight is making up a cabin cheer," said Daisy. "Every cabin has to do a cheer at the first campfire, two days from now."

She gave us a few minutes to think, then asked who had any ideas for a cheer. Carol Ann raised her hand and waved it around like kids do in school when they really, really know an answer. Daisy called on her. Carol Ann stood up and read a whole cheer from a sheet of paper. It went like this:

Mohawk cabin is our name.
Going camping is our game.
If you don't like us, that's a shame.
'Cause Mohawk is the cabin of fame.

We all voted to use Carol Ann's cheer. I think she wrote it before she even got to camp.

When it was lights out, which means time to go to bed, Daisy said, "Good night, sweet ladies," then went to her bed to read. I checked my bunk for snakes, rubbed Bug-B-Gone insect-repellent lotion all over me, then got inside my sleeping bag with Jingle Bell.

The pillow on the bunk smelled funny, so I rolled over on my back and listened to Carol Ann in the bunk above me talk about how she wanted us to win the Cabin-of-the-Week Award. She stuck her head down over the side of the bunk. Her curly yellow hair bounced around her upside-down face as she said, "Last year my cabin didn't win because some people didn't care. But this year I'm going to win. I mean, we're going to win. I bet we get points for the best cheer."

I looked over at Skye. She was curled up with her face toward the wall. One of her ponytails, the small one, had come undone.

I think she was still crying. I knew how she felt.

"Good night, Skye," I said.

"Good night," she snuffled.

Before I went to sleep, I turned on my flashlight and hung it from a nail on the side of my bunk. I wrote a letter home:

Dear Mom and Dad and Philip,

I miss you very, very, very, very, very, very, very much. Camp is scary. I feel like crying every minute. The bathrooms are gross. I saw a spider near the sink when I was washing up for bed. I think it was looking at me. I am not going to the bathroom during the night, even if I explode.

I want to go home real bad.
So does Jingle Bell. Skye doesn't
like camp either. I ate a lot of
watermelon pits at supper because
I was scared to spit them out
in front of everybody.
                    Love,
                        Beany
P.S. I forgot to pack my toothbrush.

I turned off my flashlight and hugged
Jingle Bell and cried. I tried to cry real quiet
so Carol Ann wouldn't hear.

Swim Test

★ ★ ★
★ ★ ★

The next morning someone playing a bugle very loud outside our cabin woke us up. At camp they use bugles instead of alarm clocks. I made my bed, put on some Bug-B-Gone lotion, and went to the showers.

I was scared to take a shower. The shower room was kind of dark and kind of yucky. It had a gray cement floor and gray walls with tiny windows way up high. There was just one light hanging from the ceiling in the middle of the room, so I knew that if I went into a shower stall and there was a bug in there, I wouldn't see it till it tried to attack me. My only hope was that the Bug-B-Gone would work, like on the TV commercials.

There were six shower stalls, and when I got there a few girls were already in line to use them. As I waited my turn, I decided I would ask my parents to send me a hat with a light on it, like miners wear, so I could take a shower and look for bugs at the same time.

Every time I got to be first in line I let the person behind me go ahead. I figured if I waited long enough, the bugs might get washed down the drains. Finally, I was the last one there. Just as I was peeking inside the shower curtain, the loud bugle started playing again to let everyone know it was time for breakfast. I turned and ran back to my cabin. I put on some shorts and my Camp Onondaga T-shirt as fast as I could. When I sat down on my bunk to check inside my sneakers for spiders before putting them on, I saw that Skye was curled up on her bunk facing the wall, just like the night before, only now she was dressed. Her hair was not in ponytails. "Aren't you going to breakfast?" I asked.

"I'm not hungry," she said.

"I'm very hungry," I said. "But I think it's late, so I'm kind of scared to walk into the mess hall alone."

Skye rolled over and looked at me. Her face was all red and blotchy, like she'd been crying again.

"You're scared?" she asked.

"Yeah," I said. "I feel like everybody's going to look at me when I walk in."

"Maybe we could walk in together,"

Skye said, sitting up. She smoothed down her hair and asked, "Do I look okay?"

"Um-hmm," I said, trying not to look at her puffed-up, red eyes.

When we walked into the mess hall, everyone else was already eating. But the minute they saw us, people started to clap and yell out:

You're late, you're late.
We'll wait, we'll wait.
You've got until the count of eight
To find an empty seat and plate.

Then they started to count real loud. Skye and I had to race up and down the rows of tables as fast as we could, looking for an empty place. I didn't know what would happen if they got to eight and we were still standing, but I didn't want to find out. Carol

Ann had saved a space for me between her and Megan. Carol Ann was waving at me like crazy, but I let Skye take the seat next to her. Right on the count of eight I found an empty seat at a table full of boys.

Breakfast was awful. A huge bowl full of little boxes of cereal had been put on the table, but by the time I got there the only cereal left was shredded wheat. The boys at my table called it dreaded wheat. It tasted like wet string. The boys burped a lot. But I have a brother, so it wasn't a problem.

After breakfast we had flag raising, then cabin check, which means the camp director comes into each cabin to see if everybody made their beds look neat and put away their clothes. My pajama top was on the floor, sticking out a little bit from under my bed on account of me being in such a hurry to get dressed that morning, so we didn't get a perfect score of 100. We got 95.

When the director left, Carol Ann turned to me and said, "You probably lost us points by being late for breakfast." Then she ran out of the cabin, calling, "Hey, Megan, wait for me!" I put on my bathing suit and hurried to the lake to take a swimming test. I didn't want to be late for that and have everybody count to eight again.

Each camper has to take a swimming test the first day so the leaders can figure out which kids might drown. There were a bunch of swim teachers in the water, testing the kids one by one. When it came my turn, I could do a lot of the stuff my teacher, Mr. Burr, asked me to do, like floating, and breathing while I swam. But when he asked if I could dive, I told him I didn't know how.

I worry that diving will make a lot of water go up my nose. I worry that if I try to dive I might go all the way to the bottom and then run out of breath before I get back to the top of the water. I worry that I won't even be able to find my way back to the top.

Mr. Burr told me that even though I didn't dive, I was good enough to go in the deep water. That was because of all the swimming lessons my mom made me take at the Y.

After my swimming test, I noticed that Skye hadn't taken hers yet. She was doing what I did in the shower that morning, letting everyone go ahead of her. Finally she was the last person.

A swim teacher took Skye into shallow water and told her to put her face in the water. Skye kept saying, "Just a minute, I'm not ready."

So the teacher said, "How about if I do it first?" She stuck her face in the water. "Now it's your turn," she said.

But Skye still kept repeating, "Just a minute, I'm not ready."

"I'll help you," said the teacher, and she put her hand on the back of Skye's head. "Hold your breath." Then the teacher gen-

tly pushed Skye's face into the water. Skye pulled it right out, sputtering and coughing.

"Good job!" said the teacher. "Tomorrow we'll work on keeping it in the water for a count of five." After that, Skye sat on the beach for the rest of swim time.

That afternoon, during the time called fun swim, which means you can do anything you want in the water, Skye just sat on the beach. Every time I looked at Skye from the water, I felt bad. I wished she could be having fun like I was, playing water tag with Kwaneesha and Tory. That's when I got the idea that I would help Skye not be scared of the water.

When it was free time, I put on some more Bug-B-Gone, then looked for Skye. She wasn't curled up on her bunk, and she wasn't on the cabin porch, where some of the girls were making friendship bracelets out of colored thread and beads. I finally found her sitting under a tree behind our cabin, pulling up grass one blade at a time.

"Want a Ho-Ho?" I asked. My parents had packed a surprise in my duffel bag, a box of ten Hostess Ho-Hos, which I figured would last me almost all week if I ate two a day. I was going to eat one during free time in the afternoon and one at night, since I didn't have to worry about brushing my teeth after eating sweets. But sitting under the tree, I decided Skye needed a Ho-Ho more than I did.

"No, thanks," she said, when I told her about my stash.

"I'm sorry about breakfast," I said, sitting down next to her.

"No problem," she said.

"I'm sorry about your swim test," I said.

"No problem," she answered.

"Have you ever taken swim lessons before?" I asked.

"No."

"Your mom didn't make you go, huh?"

"I don't have a mom."

"Who takes care of you?"

"My dad."

"He packs your lunch and drives you places and everything?"

"Yeah." Right away I remembered her

crooked ponytails the day she came to camp. I wondered if her dad made the part in her hair.

"Does your dad tell dumb jokes?" I asked.

"No."

"My dad does. Want to hear one?"

Skye nodded.

"What goes tick-tock, bow-wow, tick-tock?"

"What?"

"A watchdog."

I think Skye smiled a little.

"Do you have brothers or sisters?" I asked.

"No, it's just me and my dad. We live in an apartment."

"Does it have a fire escape?"

"Yeah," she said.

"You're lucky."

I asked Skye to wait there for a minute. I went inside our cabin to get two Ho-Hos. When I came back out and put one in her lap, she took it. As we ate our Ho-Hos, I asked, "Do you want me to help you not be afraid of the water?"

"Shh," said Skye.

So I whispered, "Do you want me to?"

"Shh," she said again, leaning forward and turning her head to the side. "Listen."

I shut my eyes and tried to listen as hard as I could. At first all I could hear was kids playing basketball. Then I heard, "Cheep, cheep." In a tree not far away, Skye and I saw a nest of baby birds.

"I wonder if the mother bird is around," Skye said. In a few minutes the mother bird flew to her babies with a big worm in her mouth. They ate the gross worm like it was the best meal in the world.

After the mother bird flew away, I told Skye my plan to help her not be afraid of the water.

"Follow me," I said. We went to the mess hall kitchen. Mrs. Mueller, the lady in charge of the kitchen, was busy chopping up carrots. She did it so fast I thought she might chop off part of her finger, and I decided I would not eat the salad that night. I asked her if she had a big pan.

"Yah," she said. "And what for are you geddles needing it?" Mrs. Mueller talked a

little different from us. *Yah* meant "yes." And when she said *girls,* it came out sounding like "geddles." We found out later that she talked that way because she came from a place called "the old country." I told her I needed the pan for a swimming lesson.

"And what is learning to swim, a little mouse?" Mrs. Mueller laughed and gave us a big silver pan with handles.

"Tomorrow I make spaghetti, so you geddles get it back to me by then, yah?" We promised and crossed our hearts. We filled the pan with water, right up to the top, and carried it behind our cabin.

"Put just your chin in the water like this," I said, and I did it first to show her how easy it was. Skye put in her chin. Next I put in my chin and mouth. Skye did that, too.

"Now here's the hard part. Hold your breath and put in your chin, your mouth,

and your nose. It's only a pan of water, so
you can't drown or anything."

By the time the bugle played for supper,
Skye had put her whole face in the water.
She kept it there for the count of five, then
lifted it out, sputtering and smiling.

"Tomorrow when you do it in the lake, just pretend you're doing it in the spaghetti pan," I said.

After supper, we all sat in a circle on the cabin floor, waiting for Daisy to start our cabin meeting. Skye was on one side of me and Megan was on the other. Next to Megan was Carol Ann, who had left a space next to her so Daisy would sit there.

While we waited, Carol Ann leaned across Megan and said to me, "Hey, Beany, did you see me dive during my swim test today?" She said it loud so everyone heard.

Then Megan said, "Your dive was awesome, Carol Ann! I wish I could dive like that. Don't you Beany?"

"I guess so," I said.

"You should work on learning to dive this week," Carol Ann said to me. "That would be a good goal, and I bet the leaders would give our cabin points for something big like that." When I didn't answer, Carol Ann said, "Isn't that a good idea?"

"Yeah," I said, just so Carol Ann would stop talking about it.

Daisy came in with a clipboard and squeezed herself between Fiona and Kwaneesha. First, she told us our point total. When she said that our cabin was in sixth place, Carol Ann gave me a mad look.

Next, we practiced our cabin cheer, the one Carol Ann had made up. Carol Ann showed us how to do some clapping and foot stomping and arm waving to go with the cheer. She had learned how to do cheers from her sister, who is a cheerleader in high school.

Finally, Daisy looked at her clipboard and asked if anyone had any announcements to make before she closed the meeting.

"I do," said Carol Ann. She stood up. "I just want to tell everyone that Beany is going to try to dive by the end of the week. I bet it'll get our cabin zillions of points." Then Carol Ann started to clap, and everyone joined in.

I almost started to cry, but I put my head down and recited the times tables inside my head to stop me from doing it. I was so mad at Carol Ann and her big mouth. All she cared about was winning Cabin of the Week.

At lights out, Daisy said, "Good night, sweet ladies," and went to her bed to read. I put on some Bug-B-Gone and got into bed. I turned on my flashlight and hung it from a nail. Quietly, I reached under my bunk for a Ho-Ho. Just as I got it unwrapped and was about to take a bite, Carol Ann's hand came

down from the bunk above and waved back
and forth.

"What?" I asked.

"You know what," said Carol Ann.

"No, what?" I asked.

"Share."

So I had to get another Ho-Ho and hand
it up to Carol Ann.

After I ate my Ho-Ho, I wrote a letter
home:

Dear Mom and Dad and Philip,

I miss you very, very, very, very much. I want to come home.

Camp is not fun, except for the swimming part. There are a lot of bugs here. At night there are scary noises under my cabin. Carol Ann is mean. I'm supposed to dive by the end of the week so we can win the camp award, but I can't do it.

I'm helping Skye put her head in a pail of water.

I hope you didn't pay too much money for me to go to camp. It's not worth it. I wish you spent the money for a horse instead.

Love,

Beany

P.S. I still haven't brushed my teeth. I did not take a shower either.

P.S.S. I need a hat with a light on top.

I turned off my flashlight. I cried, but just a little. I put my face in my pillow when I needed to sniffle.

After a few minutes, Daisy put out the tiny light that hung over her bed. She walked around the room, peeking into each bunk. When she came to mine, she leaned down, so her head was close to mine. Her breath smelled like peppermint.

"My spies tell me you're helping Skye," Daisy whispered. "You're a sweet little bean." Then she scratched Jingle Bell behind the ear and left. Jingle Bell and I like Daisy a lot. I would never play tricks on her like Philip said to do.

Campfire

★ ★ ★
★ ★

The next morning I jumped out of my bunk the minute the bugle music started. I put on Bug-B-Gone, ran to the showers and didn't let anyone move ahead of me in line. No matter how scary the shower was, getting to breakfast late was worse.

When I got into the shower, I saw a black blob on the wall. It might have been a spot, or it might have been a giant bug, but it wasn't moving, so I just kept far away from it and took the quickest shower I bet anyone has taken in the whole history of the world.

I ran back to my cabin to put on some more Bug-B-Gone, then raced for the mess hall. I was the first person to get there. I took a seat at the very end of a table so I could get first pick of the cereal. But when the big bowl with the boxes of cereal was put on the table, it was put at the other end.

All that was left by the time it got to me was dreaded wheat and something called muesli. I didn't want to take a chance on something with a weird name like muesli, so I took the dreaded wheat. Carol Ann made up a cheer for the people in the kitchen:

We won't eat
Dreaded wheat.
We want sugar-coated cereal,
'Cause that's fun to eat.

She wanted everybody at our table to clap and do the cheer, but nobody would.

On the way to morning swim lesson, Skye seemed a little nervous, so I told her another one of my dad's dumb riddles.

"Why did the elephants get thrown out of the swimming pool?"

Skye shrugged.

"Because they couldn't keep their trunks up."

At Skye's lesson, when the swim teacher told her to put her face in the water, Skye did it! The teacher looked surprised. By the end of class, Skye could hold her breath under water for almost the count of ten. The teacher gave her a high-five and hugged her.

My swim didn't go so well. At the end of the lesson, Carol Ann told Mr. Burr I wanted to learn to dive. "Do you, Beany?" he asked me. I didn't want to say no, with Carol Ann right there, so I just shrugged my shoulders. So he took me out to the floating wooden raft that people dive off. I stood on the raft. I even went right up to the edge. Mr. Burr explained how to dive.

Carol Ann came up next to me and said, "Like this. Watch." Then she dived off, making a big splash and causing the float to rock back and forth. But I got all fluttery and quivery when I leaned over and looked down into the water. It looked so dark and deep. I couldn't even see the bottom. I backed away from the edge.

"That's okay, Beany," said Mr. Burr. "Diving is a big step. It takes time."

After swimming I had arts-and-crafts. The teacher had us make hats for the hat contest to be held at the campfire that night.

I was starting to worry about the campfire. It seemed like one big contest. We had to do our cheer and show our hats in front of all the other campers. The leaders told us nobody had to do any of the stuff; we should only do what we wanted to. I guess the leaders didn't know about Carol Ann.

Skye was in the same arts-and-crafts class as me. She sat down next to me and whispered, "Let's make our hats real fast so we can leave early and go watch our baby birds." When we finished, the teacher looked at our hats, but didn't say they were good, like she said to some of the kids. Then she told us we were excused.

We got two Ho-Hos, I put on some Bug-B-Gone, and we went to sit under the tree behind our cabin to watch the birds. They were very loud for being so little. They chirped and kept their mouths open, hoping for some food. The mother bird did bring home some worms.

"Should we feed them? I've got a little bit of a Ho-Ho left," I said to Skye.

But Skye didn't think we should get near the birds. She said the mother would not like that. So we watched and hoped the mother would come. We watched for a long time, but she didn't come.

After a while Skye said, "Beany, are you still scared being at camp?"

"Yeah," I said. "Are you?"

"Yeah. I hate swimming class. And I miss my dad."

"I miss my bed and my pillow and my cereal," I said.

We watched the birds for a while longer, then went to lunch.

★ ★ ★

During fun swim that afternoon I helped
Skye in the water some more. Daisy did,
too. We taught Skye the kind of floating
where you lay face down on top of the
water with your arms straight out in front of
you. My brother calls it "dead man's float,"
but I didn't tell Skye that.

"Just pretend you're in a giant spaghetti pot," I told Skye. Daisy held Skye up under the stomach and I held up Skye's legs.

Daisy said, "Trust us, hon. We won't let go."

I was a little worried that Skye might ask me why I wanted her to float, while I wasn't brave enough to try to dive. She didn't, though. I think she knew it was different.

Skye only said, "Just a minute, I'm not ready," a few times. Then she took a big breath and did it!

During afternoon free time, Skye and I went to the kitchen to return the spaghetti pot. While we washed the pot, we noticed that Mrs. Mueller was mumbling to herself and wiping sweat off her forehead every few seconds.

"Are you okay?" Skye asked her.

"Ach, I would be if I had four hands and

rolling skates for feet," she said. "One of my workers just went home sick."

"We can help," said Skye.

"We?" I whispered to her. "I don't know how to cook food; I only know how to eat it."

"I fix supper for me and my dad lots of times," Skye said. "It's easy."

Mrs. Mueller told us to wash our hands, put on plastic gloves, and put net things over our hair. She said that was a law. The net thing was ugly, but I didn't want to go to jail, so I put it on. Then she showed us how to scoop meat out of a big bowl, using an ice cream scooper, and roll the meat into meatballs. It was fun. Mrs. Mueller gave each of us a brownie when we were finished.

When we got back to our cabin, Carol Ann was standing on the porch waiting for us with her hands on her hips.

"Where have you been? Didn't you see the note I put on the bulletin board about meeting at four o'clock to practice for the campfire tonight?" she said. "You missed the whole practice."

Carol Ann held the screen door open for us, then stomped behind us into the cabin. First she made us show her the hats we

made in class that morning. Mine was made
of construction paper shaped into a cone
with cotton balls glued all over it. Skye's was
a construction paper cone with leaves glued
all over it. Carol Ann just sighed when she
saw them. Her hat was awesome! It looked
like an Indian chief's hat, with long feathers
sticking up and some fake fur around the
edges and strips of leather hanging down at
the sides.

"Where'd you get all the feathers?" Skye asked.

"I brought them from home. We made hats at camp last year, so I brought supplies, just in case we did it again." She glanced at my hat, then said, "It's a good thing I did, too."

When it was finally time to go to the campfire that night, I was nervous. Carol Ann, Megan, and Kwaneesha, who'd all been at Camp Onondaga the year before, told us what the campfires were like.

"They're big!" Carol Ann said. I already knew that because I'd seen the pile of logs set up earlier that day.

"We call them Rice Krispie fires," said Kwaneesha, "because they snap, crackle, and pop."

"After the campfire, everybody comes

back smelling like smoke," said Megan.

I wondered how hot the fire would be and if sparks would fly out of it and burn me. I wondered if there would be a lot of smoke going in my eyes. I put on Bug-B-Gone and brought a squeeze bottle filled with water, just in case I caught on fire.

The campfire was enormous. It crackled and spit out sparks, but we all sat on logs far away from it, so we didn't have to worry about getting burned or breathing smoke. The logs went halfway around the fire in rows. Each row of logs was higher than the one in front of it. It reminded me of the movies, where the rows of seats go up higher and higher.

The first thing we did was the Camp Onondaga cheer. Then the camp counselors taught us a funny song about someone finding a peanut, and cracking it open and eating it even though it was rotten, and getting sick. Then each of us had to model our hats. The counselors picked the ten best ones. The people with the ten best ones stood up and the rest of us clapped. Whoever got the loudest clapping won.

Carol Ann's hat was in the top ten, but she didn't win. The winning hat was made of soda cans glued together in a pyramid. I think we clapped so hard because of all the soda the kid had to drink to make the hat.

Next, every cabin did their cheer. We did our cheer the way we'd practiced, with the clapping and stomping and arm waving. I decided our cheer might win. Some of the other cheers didn't even rhyme.

While the counselors were deciding which five cabins had the best cheer, everyone from our cabin sat with our fingers crossed and our arms crossed and our legs

crossed. Carol Ann even told us to keep our eyes crossed, but mine started to feel funny, so I had to uncross them. When the camp director was about to announce the winning cheers, Carol Ann grabbed my arm and hung onto it and kept saying, "Please, please, please," and "I hope, I hope, I hope."

Her "pleases" and "I hopes" and all the crossing we did worked! We had one of the five best cheers! When the campfire ended, we went back to our cabin yelling our cheer, even Daisy.

Right before lights out, Daisy said, "I'm proud of all of you, and not just because of having a good cheer or cool hats. Today I saw and heard about some really nice and really special things some of you have been doing."

Carol Ann whispered to me, "I held the screen door open for her when we went out to the campfire."

Then Daisy said, "Good night, sweet ladies," and went to her bed to read.

After lights out, I tried to open up a Ho-Ho inside my sleeping bag so Carol Ann wouldn't hear. But just as I was about to take my first bite, Carol Ann's hand came

down again. I had to give her my last Ho-
Ho.

Before I went to sleep I wrote a letter
home.

Dear Mom and Dad and Philip,

I miss you very, very, very much. I want to come home.

I still don't like camp, except for Skye and Daisy and the baby birds and campfire. I like the nurse, too. She dresses all in white even her shoes. Whenever I pass by her office I see her sitting at her desk all alone. After lunch today I snuck into her office and put some flowers on her desk.

Today I held Skye's legs up
and made a hat and some meatballs.
Love,
Beany

P.S. I have not brushed my
teeth in three days. I hope
they don't fall out. But I
took a shower, even with a
blob on the wall.
P.S.S. I used up all my
Bug-B-Gone and Ho-Hos.
Please send more.
P.S.S.S. Do not send peanuts.

Campout

★ ★ ★
★ ★ ★

By Wednesday our cabin was in fifth place
for points. On Thursday after cabin check,
Daisy told us our cabin had moved up to
third place. We all cheered. Then she told us
that we were going on an overnight hike
into the woods, where we would sleep in
tents. I did not cheer. Daisy told us to pack
anything we'd need for overnight and be
ready to go right after lunch.

Carol Ann was all excited, talking about
how we were going to be like explorers.

"Maybe we'll see a bear!" she said as we packed our duffel bags. She said it like seeing a bear was a good thing, instead of something that would make you scream your head off and then faint, at which time the bear would eat you.

I knew Jingle Bell was not going to like sleeping in the woods, so I put him in the bottom of my bag, where he couldn't see where he was going. On top of him I put pajamas, sunscreen, sunglasses, my first-aid kit just in case I got bitten by a snake, my flashlight, extra batteries, and a towel. I asked Skye if she had any Bug-B-Gone, but she didn't. I wished I had a Ho-Ho to pack.

After we were packed, we had our swim lessons and Skye did some more floating with her face in the water. The teacher wanted her to kick her legs, too, but Skye wouldn't do it. Mr. Burr asked me if I wanted to work on diving, but I said I'd rather keep practicing swimming on my back. When the lesson was over, I rushed out of the water and ran back to my cabin before Carol Ann could find me and make me try to dive.

After swim lesson was archery class. At my first archery class I had found out that *archery* means shooting a bow and arrow. The teacher had shown us how to hold the bow and arrow and had told us to aim at a big square clump of hay that had a target on it. We were supposed to aim for the red circle in the middle of the target.

At this class we had to practice aiming for the target some more. I was not a good archery-ist. I could never pull the bow back far enough, and my arrows kept falling out of the bow. I never even got one arrow close to the target. They always landed on the ground right in front of my feet. Fiona, from my cabin, was in my archery class and couldn't shoot very well either.

"The only thing we'll end up hitting is our toes," she said.

After archery was lunch. Then it was time to go on the campout. Even though it

was hot outside, I put on long pants and a long-sleeved shirt, just in case we walked through poison ivy. Daisy asked if there were any questions.

"Will there be bears?" I asked.

"No bears, unless some of you are bringing your stuffed ones," said Daisy. "There won't be any lions or tigers either. But there's going to be a surprise, and it *is* an animal."

Four cabins went on the trip—two boys' cabins and two girls' cabins. We hiked through the woods, trying to guess what the surprise would be, till we came to an open area where some big tents were set up. There was one tent for each cabin of kids. We had to unfold little beds called cots, made of metal and cloth, then unroll our sleeping bags onto the cots before we hiked some more to get to the surprise.

The surprise was the best thing in the whole wide world! It was horses! When I saw the saddled horses lined up and tied to a fence, I got so excited I almost screamed. I have wanted a horse ever since I visited a horse farm with the Brownie Scouts and rode on a horse named Mr. Bumble. I am even saving up to buy a horse, even though my parents tell me that's not going to happen.

We were going to ride the horses on a trail. The people who brought the horses told us the horses knew the trail and would go to the end where there was a barn and food waiting for them.

From riding Mr. Bumble in Brownies, I already knew one thing about horses—they smell kind of funny. So I didn't say *pheww* like some of the kids did when we stood near the horses and listened to the rules

about how to get on a horse and hold the reins, and about not kicking them or scaring them.

My horse was named Buttercup. When Daisy helped me put my foot in the stirrup and lifted me onto the saddle, my heart started to beat very fast. If I fell off, it was a long way down to the ground. I kept saying, "Nice Buttercup," so the horse would like me.

Skye would not get on a horse by herself, even though I told her it was not too scary. She rode with Daisy. The horses all walked in a line on the trail.

Carol Ann's horse, Lightning, was at the end, and it went so slow that she kept saying, "Giddyup." I guess the horse didn't know what *giddyup* meant because after a while, it stopped walking and just stood there. "Giddyup, Lightning. Come on, move it!" she said, real loud. But the horse turned its head and looked at her, then turned back and whinnied. I think that meant *no*. One of the guides had to take Lightning's rein to keep it moving.

When we got to the barn, we were allowed to feed our horse a carrot. Then it was time to leave. "I wish you could come home with me, Buttercup," I said. I gave Buttercup a hug. She shook her mane. I think that meant she liked me. Horseback riding was fun, except that my rear end was a little sore from bouncing up and down.

Near the horse barn was a field full of wild flowers. Before we headed back to the tents, the girls stopped to pick some flowers, while the boys ran around pretending they were horses. Brian yelled, "Look at me! I'm as fast as Lightning." Then he stopped running and stood perfectly still. We all laughed, except for Carol Ann. Then the boys ran ahead, while the girls stayed in the field and made wreaths to put in each other's hair. I saw some daisies, so I made a wreath for Daisy to wear.

When we got back to our tents, I was tired, but I couldn't wait to tell Jingle Bell about Buttercup. I looked on my sleeping bag. Jingle Bell was not there. I looked inside my sleeping bag. Jingle Bell was not

there. I looked under my sleeping bag. Jingle Bell was not there. I looked in my duffel bag. Jingle Bell was not there. I screamed.

Daisy came running in to see what was wrong. By then, other girls were yelling that their stuffed animals were gone too. Skye did not yell, though, because she didn't bring a stuffed animal to camp. She had thought kids would laugh at her if she brought one.

"Here we go again," one of the cabin counselors said. She walked over to the boys' tents. We followed her. She blew her whistle and yelled, "Get out here, on the double."

I think "on the double" means to come out fast. The boys came out of their tents. They looked at each other, grinning.

"All right, where are they?" said the counselor.

Brian pointed up into a tree. Then the boys started laughing like they had just heard the funniest joke in the whole world. But what we saw was not funny. Our stuffed animals were high up in the tree. The counselor made the boys get them, then apologize to us. As we walked away, Carol Ann yelled at the boys, "You big lunkheads!" Then she hugged her bear, Snoodles, and put him way down inside her sleeping bag.

After supper we had a small campfire and sang the rotten peanut song. We also learned a great song called "Great Green Gobs of Greasy Grimy Gopher Guts." Then we toasted marshmallows on long sticks. Carol Ann stuck her stick right into the fire and the marshmallow burned, but she ate it anyway. She cooked each marshmallow so fast she got to eat six of them.

After the campfire, we got ready for bed. Then Daisy told each of us to get out our brush or comb, and she would do our hair in French braids or do it up like movie stars. I looked around at the other girls. Most of them had hair that was long enough to put in a braid or twirl like a movie star. Tory's was almost down to her waist. My hair is short, and it will never look like a movie star's. It mostly just lays there or sometimes sticks out in weird ways.

When it was my turn, I told Daisy she could skip me. I told her no one could make my hair look good. But Daisy said, "Hon, I am planning to be a hairstylist. I can make anyone's hair look good."

She said she had a special idea for my hair. She dug around in her duffel bag and pulled out a handful of tiny hair clips shaped like butterflies. She parted my hair into little sections and put a butterfly in each part. She

gave me a mirror. When I saw myself, I couldn't stop smiling.

The only bad part of the campout, besides the boys taking our stuffed animals, was when Kwaneesha went to her cot to go to sleep and screamed, "Eeeeeyouuuuu!" There was a frog on her sleeping bag. Daisy put a little box over it and flipped the box over. She put her hand over the box and took the frog outside.

"That might have been your prince charming," Daisy said to Kwaneesha. "You should have kissed it instead of screeching. You could have been a princess."

"Yeah, sure," we said.

"Good night, sweet ladies," Daisy said and went into a corner to read with a flashlight. We didn't go to sleep. All of us, except Skye, talked and talked. Skye just listened. I told one of my dad's dumb riddles. Why do boy deer wear braces? Because they have buck teeth. Jocelyn told a spooky story about the time she heard a ghost in her grandmother's attic.

Finally Daisy said if we didn't be quiet and close our eyes, she was going to leave. So then we whispered.

The next morning we didn't wake up to loud bugle music; we woke up to loud whistle blowing.

For breakfast we were supposed to eat something the counselors called breakfast-in-a-bag. We each got a little paper bag. We put a piece of bread and a piece of bacon into the bottom. We cracked two eggs on top of that. Then we rolled the bag shut and put a stick through the top. We toasted it over the fire. When it was done we called it burned breakfast-in-a-bag. I would have

liked dreaded wheat better than that breakfast.

We got back to camp just in time for
lunch and free swim. During free swim,
Daisy and I helped Skye float some more.
We held her up while she tried to kick her
legs.

As we walked out of the water, Daisy said
to me, "I know Carol Ann wants you to
dive. But you don't have to do it if you
don't want to, hon. Don't do it just because

of Carol Ann." Daisy patted my shoulder.

Later, Skye and I helped Mrs. Mueller make pies, because her arthur-itis was bothering her.

"Did you geddles have fun on the camping out?" she asked us.

"The boys stole our stuffed animals!" I said.

"But did you have fun?"

"We ate burned eggs!" Skye said.

"Yah, but did you have fun?"

"There was a gross frog on Kwaneesha's cot!" I said.

"Yah, but you are not answering my question. Did you have fun?"

"Yes," we both said at the same time.

"Ach, I knew you would," Mrs. Mueller said, smiling.

That night, after Daisy told us, "Good night, sweet ladies," I wrote a letter.

Dear Mom and Dad and Philip,

Thank you for sending the toothbrush and Bug-B-Gone and Ho-Hos. They came today. I put a Ho-Ho under Daisy's pillow as a surprise.

Yesterday I slept in a tent. Daisy put butterflies in my hair. I ate a burned bag of eggs. I rode Buttercup. You HAVE to let me have a horse. I will DIE if I don't get one.

The baby birds are eating a lot of worms. They are fluttering their wings.

Skye kicked her feet today.

Love,
Beany

P.S. I miss you.

Last Day

★   ★
★   ★   ★   ★

On the last day of camp, right after cabin check, Daisy told us our cabin had moved up to second place for the award. She said the final points would be added up by the end of the day, and the winning cabin would be announced that night at the closing campfire.

"We have to get all the points we can today," Carol Ann said to me, "so try to be nice, especially to the camp leaders, and don't do anything dumb." Then Carol Ann reminded me that today was my last chance to try a dive.

"A dive would be so awesome, it would probably win our cabin a bunch of points and we could win!" she said, squeezing my shoulders. I didn't answer her. I went out on the porch and sat on the steps, biting my nails. Skye sat down next to me, twirling her ponytail round and round.

Then Carol Ann, Megan, Jocelyn, Kwaneesha, and Tory came out, too, to work on friendship bracelets. Daisy was on the next porch, sitting with the counselor from that cabin. They were putting on nail polish. Everyone was kind of quiet.

Gray clouds started moving toward us from far over the lake. "I wonder if they call off swimming when it rains," I said.

"No way," said Megan. "There has to be lightning and thunder before they do that."

"Did you hear something? Was that thunder?" Skye asked every few minutes.

Once I thought I saw a flash of light way out over the water, but Skye said it was my imagination. Swim lesson didn't get canceled.

That morning all the kids who couldn't swim when camp started had to take a test to see if they learned how. Skye stood in the water, shivering. I didn't know if she felt cold or nervous. "Just relax, hon," Daisy said to her.

When it was Skye's turn, she got her face wet, then did the floating part. When it was time to do everything together—the floating and the kicking and the arm paddling— Skye looked over at me. I was sitting on the floating raft. I gave her a little wave, then crossed my fingers and watched.

She took a deep breath, put her arms out

in front of her, and did it! She went from one dock to the other without sinking. I clapped and jumped up and down so hard the raft rocked, and a couple of people fell off. I jumped into the water to hug Skye.

"I did it! I did it!" she squealed.

"You did it! You did it!" I yelled. Then everybody from our cabin came over and gave her high-fives and hugged her.

My teacher asked me if I wanted to make one last try at a dive. I wanted to dive. I told myself I was going to dive. So I swam out to the floating raft, climbed up the ladder, and stood at the edge.

I leaned forward and raised my arms over my head. I looked into the dark, deep water. Then I started to shake all over. I backed away from the edge and told the teacher, "I'm not ready yet." I swam to shore.

At lunch Skye told me it was okay, that I was brave even to stand on the edge of the raft. Carol Ann patted my shoulder and said it was okay, too. But I could tell from the way she said it that I had let her down. I had let the whole cabin down.

After lunch Skye asked if I wanted to go outside to see our birds. I just wanted to lay on my bunk and rub Jingle Bell's ear, but

Skye pulled me up and outside.

We sat under our tree and watched the birds fluttering their wings and chirping. The mother was perched on a branch talking to them in bird language. All of a sudden, one of the babies started flapping its wings like crazy. Then it flew out of the nest! It didn't fly very far, just out a little, then back. Another one tried it, and then another. Skye and I looked at each other and laughed. "Go, birds!" we yelled. We were so excited, we jumped up and down and hugged each other. We ran around in big circles, flapping our arms, pretending we were the baby birds.

That afternoon, at our last free swim, I just sat on the grass and watched everyone else swim. Carol Ann dived off the raft a lot. I think she was trying to show me how easy it was.

When it was time to go back to our cabins, Daisy said, "Wait here a minute, Beany." When everyone else had gone, she said, "You've spent the whole week helping Skye. Now it's time for someone to help you." We swam out to the raft together. She asked me to stand next to her at the edge of the raft. She leaned forward. She held her arms out in front of her. She bent her knees and fell forward into the water.

Her body went in with hardly a splash. In a few seconds her head bobbed up.

"If you bend your knees and let yourself fall forward," she said, "the rest will take care of itself."

"I'm worried that a lot of water will go up my nose."

"Hold your nose with one hand and dive with the other."

"But what if I go all the way to the

bottom of the lake and don't come up?"

"You're not that heavy, so you won't go very deep. And your body will automatically come right up to the top."

"What if I need to breathe, and I'm still not at the top of the water?"

"I won't let anything happen to you, hon. I'm right here."

Finally I said, "I'm scared I'll drown."

"Hon, I haven't lost a camper yet."

Daisy told me to shake the jitters out, take a few deep breaths, and get in position.

"If you don't do it, that's all right. But if you want to try, I'm right here waiting for you. Just fall in," she said softly.

I thought of Skye swimming that morning. I thought of my baby birds flying out of the nest. I saw Daisy smiling at me. I closed my eyes, took a deep breath, and let myself fall into the water.

I felt the water rushing around my body as I went down, down into the lake. In a few seconds I started kicking my legs and came up to the top. I didn't even get out of breath.

I was so happy I started to cry. Daisy hugged me, right in the water. I climbed back onto the raft and dived again and again, till Daisy told me I was wearing out the ladder.

She put a towel around me, and we walked back to the cabin. As soon as we opened the door, Daisy yelled in, "Meet Camp Onondaga's newest diver!" Everyone cheered.

That night was the final campfire. Our parents would come to get us the next morning. As we left our cabin to go to the campfire area, Daisy gave each of us a little stick.

"You'll need them for a special ceremony at the campfire," she told us.

The fire was blazing, all red and orange. Everyone did the Camp Onondaga cheer, and each cabin did its own cheer. Then all the cabin counselors came up and did a funny play about things that had happened during the week. Skye and I being late for breakfast on the first morning was in the play. When it had happened it wasn't funny, but when the counselors did it in the play, I laughed so hard my cheeks hurt.

Then the camp director stood up. She told us what a great bunch of kids we were and how the people who worked at the camp had seen us do a lot of great things.

"You didn't know we were watching," she said. "But our spies saw everything. And we saw that most of you did a fine job of working together. We saw kindnesses that we'll never forget. We saw caring, courage, and creativity. All of you participated to your fullest. But the youngsters in one cabin did it best. They showed the spirit of Camp Onondaga at its finest. The winner is . . ." She paused and pretended she forgot the name of the winning cabin. We all groaned. Then she yelled out, "Mohawk!" Skye and I looked at each other, not believing our ears.

Carol Ann yelled, "Yes!"

We each got a certificate and a hug from Daisy. Everyone clapped and cheered.

After that, the director said, "We have a tradition here at Camp Onondaga that we'd like you to continue. We would like all of you to go to the swimming area, and as you pass by the campfire, throw your stick into the flames. Make a wish or offer a special hope for yourself as you do it."

As I walked up to the fire, I thought

about all the things that had happened to me that week. I closed my eyes, made a wish, and threw my stick into the flames.

Each of the cabin counselors lit a long torch in the fire, and we followed them to the lakeshore. They walked into the water up to their knees, forming a line. In the darkness, with only the torchlights shining on the water, they sang to us.

The sun has slowly slipped away.
And so we say good night to day.
And as the stars fill up the sky
We also say our last goodbye.
Then let us softly steal away
To sleep until the break of day.

The lake will guard you, dark and deep.
The lake will guard you as you sleep.
The trees will guard you, tall and steep.
The trees will guard you as you sleep.
The night will guard you till you rise
To say your final, sweet goodbyes.

When daylight breaks we all will part.
But you'll be with us in our heart.
Please think of us, this place, this shore
Till summer brings you back once more.

The song was so pretty it made my throat

hurt. When it ended, the counselors walked out of the water and led us back to our cabins by torch light. No one talked.

At lights out Daisy said, "Good night, sweet ladies." When she came to my bunk, she bent down to scratch Jingle Bell behind the ear. Then she put something next to my pillow. It was the butterfly hair clips. "To remember me by," she said.

"Thank you," I said, "but I'll always remember you, even without them."

When she had gone to her bed to read, I whispered to Skye, "'Night."

"'Night, Beany."

After a few minutes, Skye whispered, "Beany, are you awake?"

"Yeah."

"I'm going to miss you," she said quietly.

"I'll miss you, too," I answered.

"I don't want to spoil my wish by telling you what it was, but it had something to do with camp next year," Skye said.

"So did mine."

I smiled, hugged Jingle Bell, and fell asleep.

Have you read all of the Beany books?
☑ Check out these hilarious stories!

☐ *Don't Call Me Beanhead!*
Available in hardcover and paperback!
Meet Bernice Lorraine Sherwin-Hendricks,
also known as Beany. Beany has a tendency
to worry about things, like losing her tooth
down the drain or having enough money to
buy the latest nail polish. Will Beany ever
stop worrying and just have fun?

☐ *Beany (Not Beanhead) and the Magic Crystal*
Available in hardcover and paperback!
Interesting things always seem to happen to
Beany, like finding a magic wishing crystal.
The only problem is that the crystal grants
just one wish—and Beany can't decide what
to wish for. Should it be to win the Caring
and Sharing Contest at school, to get a
decent school picture of herself, or to have
the best birthday party ever?

☐ *Beany and the Dreaded Wedding*
When Beany's favorite cousin, Amy, asks her
to be in her wedding, Beany wants to feel
happy. Beany loves her cousin, but what a
responsibility! What if she hates her dress?
And what if she trips while EVERYONE is
watching her walk down the aisle? Eeek!

Dear Mom and Dad and Philip,

I miss you very, very, very, very, very, very, very much. I want to go home real bad. So does Jingle Bell.

Love,
Beany

Dear Mom and Dad and Philip,

I miss you very, very, very, very, very much. I want to come home. Camp is not fun, except for the swimming part. There are a lot of bugs here.

Love,
Beany